OTIS STEELE
AND THE
TAILEEBONE

OTIS STEELE
AND THE
TAILEEBONE
A Southern Tall Tale

By Tom McDermott
Illustrated by Jeff Crosby

PELICAN PUBLISHING COMPANY
GRETNA 2013

To Uncle Mac—"imagineer" of tall tales and wild spaces

*The word "Pelican" and the depiction of a pelican are
trademarks of Pelican Publishing Company, Inc.,
and are registered in the U.S. Patent and Trademark Office.*

Library of Congress Cataloging-in-Publication Data

McDermott, Tom, 1957-
  Otis Steele and the taileebone : a Southern tall tale / by Tom McDermott ;
illustrated by Jeff Crosby.
       p. cm.
  Summary: When a strange creature enters a hungry trapper's cabin, the
trapper cuts off its tail and eats it but the creature returns, determined to
retrieve its appendage.
  ISBN 978-1-4556-1736-4 (hardcover : alk. paper) -- ISBN 978-1-4556-1737-1
(e-book) [1. Stories in rhyme. 2. Monsters--Fiction. 3. Tall tales.] I. Crosby,
Jeff, ill. II. Title.
  PZ8.3.M4595474Oti 2013
  [E]--dc23
                              2012026591

Printed in Malaysia
Published by Pelican Publishing Company, Inc.
1000 Burmaster Street, Gretna, Louisiana 70053

OTIS STEELE AND THE TAILEEBONE

There was once an old trapper near Uncertain, Texas, in the piney-wood swamps and trees.

Otis Steele lived in a dog-run cabin with two bluetick hounds and not much to eat.

One night, while chewing on a stale biscuit,
Otis heard a weird, suspicious sound.
Comin' through a hole in the cabin wall
was the wildest thing he'd ever seen around.

It had big glowing eyes, long sharp claws, and strange furry ears.
And when the thing finished crawling through the hole, something even stranger appeared.

It had a thick, hairless tail that stretched across the floor and over to Otis's feet.

Otis felt the hunger rumbling in his stomach and said, "That thing looks good enough to eat!"

The dogs barked wildly as the critter bolted and gave a frightening wail.

Because Otis had taken one swing with his hatchet and caught that wild thing by its tail!

The tail flopped about as the rest of the critter ran shrieking into the woods.

But Otis took some flour and fried up that tailbone and said, "That tastes purdy good!"

He sat there gnawin' on that tailbone a while, and was feelin' full and satisfied, when he heard a weird, unfamiliar sound in the wind, blowin' just outside.

He finished off the tailbone and took his rusty hatchet over to the cabin door.

But his two brave hounds suddenly scampered off to the far side of the floor.

They hunkered against the cabin wall and whined and barked and growled.

Otis Steele put his ear up to the door and could hear the wind's strange howl.

He bent down to his knees, staying very still, when he heard a deep, frightful moan, as if someone, or something, was outside speaking, sayin' something like,

"T-a-a-a-i-i-i-l-e-e-e-b-o-n-e?
TAILEEBONE! What've you done with my
    taileebone?
Don't take what ain't yours. You should have
    known.
Just because it was lyin' there and
    looking so,
That's no reason for you to take
    my taileebone!"

Otis chased his two dogs outside and yelled,
"Go take care of that thing!"
The dogs ran off baying into the woods as
he worried what the night would bring.

Those hounds barked for an hour or more
trying to trail that wild thing up a tree.
The wind whined and howled as Otis stood
at the door, waiting anxiously.

It was about midnight when Otis heard one of his hounds yelping on the porch.

He opened the door and the dog limped inside, looking worn, beat up, and worse.

The weak hound stumbled and hid under the bed, cowerin' and whimperin'.

That's when Otis heard something at the door, scratchin' to get back in.

And someone, or something, was outside speaking in a low and frightful moan,

"T-a-a-a-i-i-i-l-e-e-e-b-o-n-e?
TAILEEBONE! What've you done with my taileebone?
Don't take what ain't yours. You should have known.
Just because it was lyin' there and looking so,
That's no reason for you to take my taileebone!"

Otis chased his dog outside, shoutin', "Get that thing; now do as I say!"
But the dog was surely smarter than Otis, 'cause it barked and ran off the wrong way.

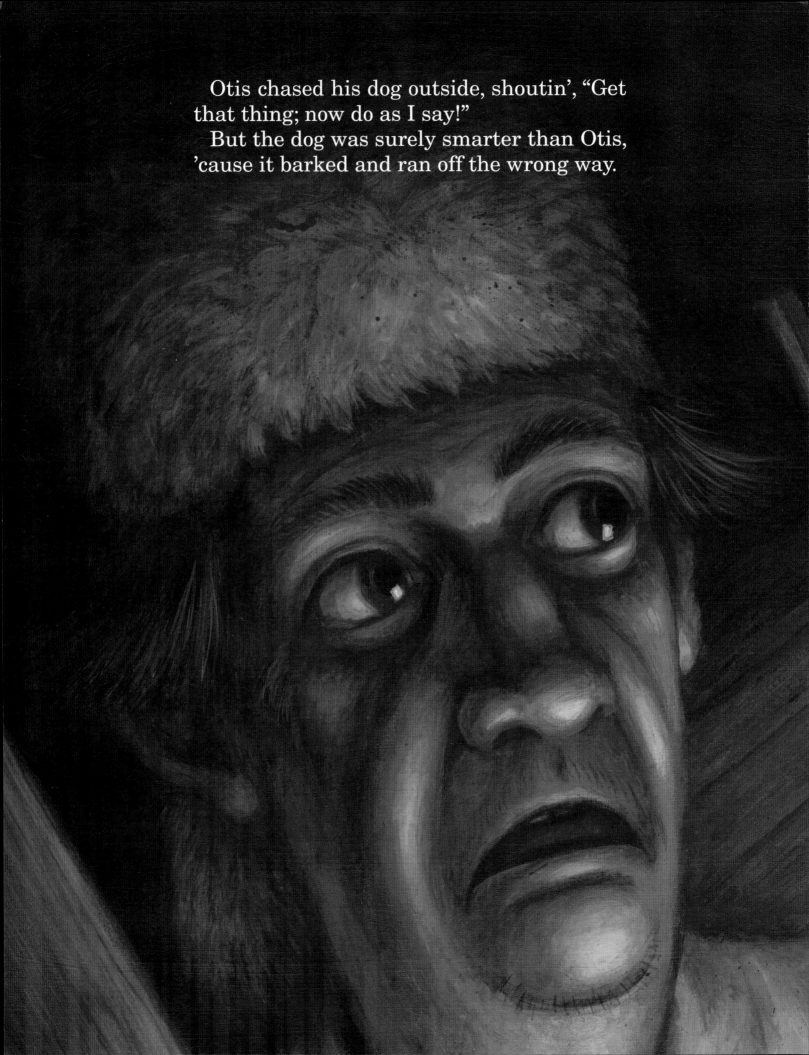

Soon all Otis could hear was the silence of
the deep, dark, swampy wood.
He looked around at his empty cabin and
shuddered and finally understood.

"I'm in trouble," he sighed, as he patched up
the hole and pulled the covers up to his chin.

He was so exhausted, he fell asleep thinkin',
"There's no way that thing can get in."

Suddenly, a chilly wind whistled through that hole as something tugged at the sheets of his bed.

And Otis awoke to see big glowing eyes, sharp claws, and that thing's furry head.

And this is what the creature said.

"*T-a-a-a-i-i-i-l-e-e-b-o-n-e?*
TAILEEBONE! What've you
done with my taileebone?
Don't take what ain't yours.
You should have known.
Just because it was lyin'
there and looking so,
That's no reason for you to
take my taileebone!"

Otis stammered to get the words out. "I, I
think I ate it—it's all gone."

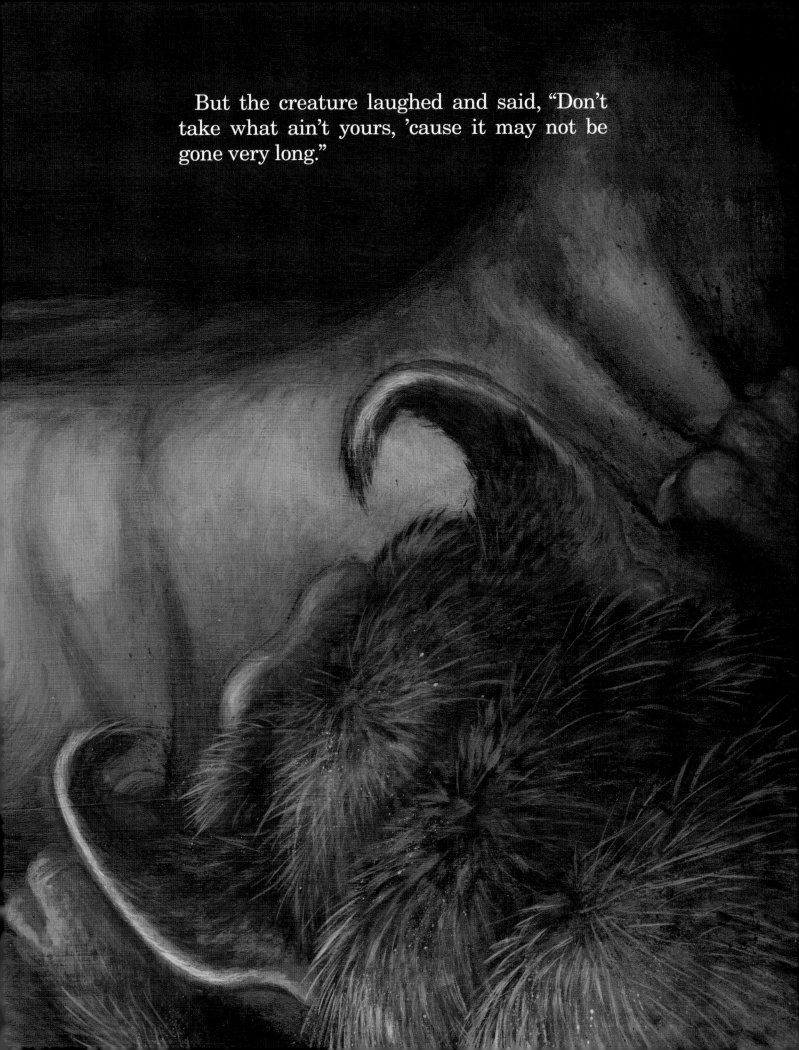

But the creature laughed and said, "Don't take what ain't yours, 'cause it may not be gone very long."

Then slowly it climbed on top of the bed,
scratchin' bedposts, blankets, and sheets.
Otis stirred and tossed under his covers,
searchin' for a quick retreat.

The creature drooled as it smiled and jumped on top of that foolish trapper.
It scratched and twisted and tugged at the sheets like there was something that it was after.

There was so much commotion as pots and
pans flew all around the old trapper's place.
A few days later, traders came looking for
Otis but they could not find any trace.

Now some folks say that Otis and his dogs simply got up and went on their way.

Others say something got into his cabin and got back what it was after that day.

But if you go out one night and set your sights on something that's not your own, you better think twice about takin' it home, 'cause you might hear somethin' like . . .

"*T-a-a-a-i-i-i-l-e-e-e-b-o-n-e?*
TAILEEBONE! What've you done with my taileebone?
Don't take what ain't yours. You should have known.
Just because it was lyin' there and looking so,
That's no reason for you to take my taileebone!"